Truth or DARE

By Luann Colombo

Troll

Thanks to my brave buddies who Dared to help me seek the Truth:
Rosemary Colombo, Kierstin Morse, Chan Lowe, Caitlin Culhane, Brandon
Colombo, Paulo Alfano, Mrs. Parmelee's sixth-grade class from Monroe Middle
School '97–'98, Catherine Kendall, Gloria Ferguson, and Andrea Anderson.

Text copyright © 1998 by Luann Colombo

Published by Troll Communications L.L.C.

Truth or Dare is produced by becker&mayer!, Kirkland, Washington
www.beckermayer.com

Design by Amy Redmond

Printed in the United States of America

ISBN 0-8167-4948-5

10 9 8 7 6 5 4 3 2 1

Introduction

Would you make a friend strut around like a chicken, or lie on the floor and sputter like bacon frying in a pan? If friends were to ask you what your most embarrassing moment was, would you tell them? You might if you were playing Truth or Dare. In this game, you'll have to share your deepest secrets with your friends—but you'll also get to make them do some ridiculous things!

Truth or Dare Swear

Before you play, everyone in the group should be sworn to secrecy. If someone decides not to be sworn to secrecy, then she or he shouldn't play. All the players must repeat the following promise:

"I swear that the secrets we tell here will stay among us. Only the person whose secret it is can grant me permission to discuss it with others. I will not tease anyone no matter how tempting it is, and I won't make anyone do something that she or he really doesn't want to do. I dare to have fun!"

Preparing to Play Truth or Dare

There are several ways to play Truth or Dare. You can follow the rules here, or make up rules of your own. Whatever you do, make sure everyone understands the rules at the beginning of the game. You will avoid lots of arguments this way.

Picking the Number

Cut out twenty small pieces of paper. Write the numbers 0 through 9 twice, one number on each piece of paper. When you're done, you should have two 0s, two 1s, two 2s, two 3s, etc. Put all the pieces of paper in a hat and mix them up. When it's your turn, reach into the hat and pick two pieces of paper. Combine the two numerals you've picked to figure out your number for that round. For example, if you first pick a 4, then pick a 2, your number would be 42.

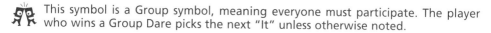 This symbol is a Group symbol, meaning everyone must participate. The player who wins a Group Dare picks the next "It" unless otherwise noted.

You can play Truth or Dare in the car! Many of the Dares can be performed in the car—just keep picking numbers until a Car Dare comes up.

The Rules
All the players sit in a circle. The oldest person playing is first to be "It." The youngest person reads the first Truth or Dare. The game starts with the first player ("It") flipping a coin: "Heads," it's a Truth; "Tails," it's a Dare. This player then draws a number from the hat. The reader reads the corresponding Truth or Dare, and the player who is "It" must answer the Truth or perform the Dare. The person to the right of the player becomes the new "It," while the person who just played becomes the reader. The game continues around the circle.

If a player gets a Truth that she or he doesn't want to answer or a Dare that she or he can't or doesn't want to do, that person can take the same number of the alternative activity. For example, if Susie draws Truth #28 and she is too embarrassed to answer it, she can choose to take Dare #28. If a player refuses to answer the Truth or do the Dare, he or she loses a turn in the next round.

Variation: Instead of flipping a coin to determine whether you get a Truth or a Dare, the Truth question is always asked first. A player can choose to answer the question or say "Dare," and the Dare of that same number is read.

Truths

1 Who is your favorite rock star? If you could go on a date with him or her, where would you go?

2 Did you ever say you were sick to stay out of school—even though you weren't? Why?

Truths

3 Have you ever burped in class? When?

4 Who do you have a crush on?

5 Would you kiss your friend to save your life?

Truths

6 What's the worst trick you've ever played on a younger kid?

7 If you could be someone else, who would it be?

8 What's the grossest thing you've ever eaten?
What's the weirdest food you've ever eaten?

9 What's the silliest article of clothing you own?
What's the most embarrassing thing your
parents made you wear?

Truths

10 Did you ever borrow (and wear) someone's clothes without telling that person? Who?

11 Did you ever find something you shouldn't have on the Internet? What was it?

Truths

12 What's the longest you've gone without taking a bath or shower?

13 Did you sleep with a security blanket or stuffed toy? Do you still have it? How old were you when you stopped using it?

Truths

14 Have you ever done someone else's homework? Have you ever let someone else do your homework? When and why?

15 Have you ever been in a fight? Who won?

Truths

16 If you could have lived during any other period in history, when would it be and why?

17 Have you ever told someone's secret after you promised you wouldn't? Why?

Truths

18 Do you think you have good judgment and make good decisions? Why? Give an example.

19 Which do you think is harder—being a girl or being a boy? Why?

Truths

20 Have you ever had the same dream more than once? What was it about?

21 Have you ever done something you truly regretted after you did it? What was it?

Truths

22 Would you go out with more than one person at a time?

23 Tell something that your mom or dad always warns you about.

Truths

24 Think of a weird situation at school and give an opinion on it.

25 Who was the first guy or girl you ever had a crush on? Who was your biggest crush?

Truths

26 If you and one other boy or girl in your grade could be the last two people on Earth, who would you choose?

27 What's the most embarrassing thing you've ever done?

Truths

28 Have you ever taken anything that didn't belong to you? What was it? Did you get caught?

29 How many times a day do you look in the mirror?

Truths

Truths

Truths

35 Have you ever cheated on a test? What happened?

36 If you could talk to someone famous, who would it be? What would you say?

Truths

44 The boy (or girl) your best friend likes asks you out—do you go?

45 Would you rather be rich or beautiful? Why?

46 What is your deepest secret?

Truths

47 If you ripped your new shirt doing something you weren't supposed to be doing, what (if anything) would you tell your mom or dad?

Truths

37 Have you ever eaten something you didn't like just to be polite? What was it?

38 What do you want to be when you grow up?

Truths

39 If you could take only five things to a desert island, what would they be (other than the survival stuff like food, water, clothes, and a sleeping bag)?

Truths

40 Would you go on a mission to Mars if you weren't sure you could ever come back? What if you couldn't come back for a year?

41 Have you ever been slobbered on by an animal? When?

Truths

42 If you could pick another country to be from, what would it be? (What about another planet?)

43 If you saw that someone you hated was in danger, would you help him or her?

Truths

44 The boy (or girl) your best friend likes asks you out—do you go?

45 Would you rather be rich or beautiful? Why?

46 What is your deepest secret?

Truths

47 If you ripped your new shirt doing something you weren't supposed to be doing, what (if anything) would you tell your mom or dad?

Truths

48 Your grandma gives you a new outfit and you hate it—do you tell her? Do you wear it to school? Do you wear it when you visit her?

49 Where would you go on your dream vacation? Who would you take with you?

Truths

50 A classmate has wicked, gross, knock-you-over bad breath—do you tell him or her?

51 Have you ever told on a friend to a parent or teacher? Why?

Truths

Truths

55 Finish this sentence: "I like my dad because..."

56 Finish this sentence: "I like my mom because..."

Truths

57 Have you ever spied on a family member? When?

58 Have you ever snooped for a gift at holiday or birthday time? If you found it, did you unwrap it?

Truths

59 Have your parents ever embarrassed you? How?

60 What is your favorite movie? How many times would you see a movie that you like?

Truths

61 What is your favorite nickname? What is your least favorite nickname?

62 Would you tell a white lie to spare someone's feelings?

Truths

63 When you're late for school, do you make up an excuse or tell the truth?

64 What do you spend your allowance on? Would you buy something popular even though you didn't like it?

Truths

65 How far would you go to get something you really want?

66 Would you take a little brother or sister out with your friends?

Truths

67 What would you do if your brother or sister embarrassed you in public?

68 How do you react to criticism (or being yelled at)?

Truths

Truths

72 Do most adults treat you like a grown-up or a child?

73 Did you ever make up an excuse for not doing your homework? When?

Truths

77 Would you defend a friend if you heard someone talking about him or her?

78 If you really liked someone even though he or she was ugly or unpopular, would you go out with him or her?

Truths

79 Do you stay mad at someone for a long time?

80 You and your good friend have a fight—who calls whom first?

81 Are you reliable? Why do you think so?

Truths

82 Can you admit when you're wrong? Can you think of a good example?

83 When someone tells you to do something just as you are about to do it anyway, you...?

Truths

84 What are your hobbies?

85 What's the best advice anyone ever gave you?

86 Is there anyone you really hate? Who?

Truths

87 What are words or phrases that you use too much?

88 Would you be a boy/girl for a week if you had the chance? How do you think you'd act differently than you do as a girl/boy?

Truths

89 What's the coolest thing you've ever experienced?

90 What's the dumbest thing you've ever done?

91 What do you like to do in the summer?

92 What character traits do you look for in a romantic boyfriend (or girlfriend)? What character traits do you look for in a platonic friend?

Truths

93 Would you go bungee jumping? Sky diving? Scuba diving?

94 Do you watch any cartoons? Which ones?

95 What do you like to collect?

Truths

96 Have you ever let someone else take the blame for something you did? When?

97 If you could go out with anyone in the world, who would it be?

Truths

98 What comic strip character are you most like?

99 Have you ever sent someone a love letter?

DARES

1 Strut around and pretend you're a chicken.

2 Run around the house (or block) loudly singing a song chosen by the group.

3 E-mail a knock-knock joke to someone.

DARES

4 Eat weird food chosen by the group (like pickles and ice cream, or mustard and chocolate).

5 Hold a pencil with the inside of your elbows and write your name on a piece of paper.

6 Hold a pencil between your knees and write "DARE."

 **7** Count backward from one hundred by threes.

8 Pat your head and rub your belly while saying a jump-rope rhyme.

9 Hop on one foot and whistle "Mary Had a Little Lamb."

 **10** Touch your tongue to your nose, or wiggle your nose.

11 Spoon-feed a member of the group.

 **12** Sing a commercial jingle.

DARES

13 Do an impression of Elvis Presley. If you don't know who he is, go ask a grown-up.

14 Sing a song with colors in it.

15 Sing a song about a duck.

DARES

16 Tell a parent (or a member of the group who pretends to be a parent) that she or he looks very nice today.

17 Walk around the room with a balloon or book between your knees. If you drop it, you have to start over.

DARES

18 Walk up and down the stairs with a book balanced on your head. If you drop it, you have to start over.

19 Using pig Latin, ask a grown-up for a peanut butter sandwich. If he or she understands you, you have to make one and eat it.

DARES

20 Kiss a dark-haired person on the cheek.

21 Walk around the room for two minutes blindfolded or with your eyes closed.

22 Whisper to the person next to you the name of someone you have a crush on.

23 Call the person you like on the phone, tell him or her who you are, and ask what time it is.

24 Act out a role from a movie that the group chooses.

25 Recite a poem.

26 Wear your shirt (clothes) backward for one hour.

27 Sing the Barney song—like you mean it.

28 Tell the group what you would write in an anonymous love letter to the person you like.

29 Pretend you're a dog. Bark and "mark" a pretend fire hydrant.

30 Do squats (deep knee bends) while balancing a cookie or a spoon on your nose.

31 Draw out a message to someone in the room using only pictures, not words, letters, or numbers. The person has to guess your message.

32 Ask a parent (or the driver) to put on loud rock music.

33 Think of a gadget you use in the kitchen (toaster, blender, etc.). Pretend you're using that gadget. The person who guesses what you are doing gets to pick the next "It."

DARES

34 Beg the person next to you for forgiveness.

35 Say the alphabet backward.

36 Stuff as many marshmallows or cookies in your mouth as you can. Eat them.

37 Curl your tongue.

38 Wiggle your ears.

39 Let someone "fix" your hair and wear it that way for the rest of the game (or party).

DARES

40 Say a tongue twister fast, five times. If you mess up, you have to take another dare. Try one of these twisters: "Rubber baby buggy bumper"; "Sally sells sea shells by the sea shore"; "I slit a sheet. A sheet I slit. Upon a slitted sheet I sit."

41 Name five movie stars in thirty seconds.

42 Have the group stand in a circle. Hold an orange under your chin and pass it to the person next to you without using your hands. Continue passing the orange from chin to chin. The first person to drop the orange is "It."

43 Sit in a dark room with all the players and tell a ghost story.

DARES

44 How many words can you make out of the letters in the next holiday of the year (Easter, Valentine's Day, etc.)? The one with the most words chooses the next "It."

45 Burp! (Make a forced burp noise.)

DARES

46 Name three things you can do to be a better person.

47 Say three overused slang words or phrases (like "As if!" or "Duh").

48 Close your eyes (don't peek!) and have someone put a small object in your hand. Describe it.

49 Get down on one knee and compliment one of the people in the room for one minute. (Car Dare: Skip the knee part and compliment one of the people in the car for one minute.)

DARES

50 Do an impression of your teacher (or another adult).

51 Sit cross-legged on the floor with your arms up over your head, then slowly lower your arms to the floor chanting: "Oh Wa, Ta Goo, Si Am."

52 Do a Hawaiian hula dance—don't forget to hum along.

53 Roll a peanut across the floor with your nose.

54 Figure out what three to the fifth power is.

55 Name the squares and cubes of the numbers one through ten.

56 Act out the title of a book and let the group guess it. The person who guesses it first gets to pick the next "It."

57 Name a noun, pronoun, and adjective. Use them all in one sentence.

DARES

58 Juggle three like objects (tennis balls, oranges, etc.).

 **59** Keep your eyes closed for what you think is a minute while someone times you.

DARES

60 Stare down the person next to you. The first to blink (or laugh) has to do the next Dare.

61 Using a roll of toilet paper, have the group dress you like a bride and parade you around the house. Don't forget the bouquet and veil.

62 Make eye contact with a passenger in a passing car. Make that person laugh.

63 Start timing using a clock or watch with a second hand and stop timing after a while. When you stop, the group must guess how much time has passed. The person who comes closest is the winner and gets to pick the next "It."

64 In front of a parent, discuss an incident that happened at school. If no parent is present, have a member of your group pretend to be a parent.

65 You have sixty seconds to make the person next to you laugh. The "winner" chooses the next "It."

66 Sing the last song you had stuck in your head.

67 Go outside in your pajamas and skip around the driveway while your friends watch.

68 Act out a task you've done for your teacher. Let the group guess the task. The person who guesses correctly gets to pick the next "It."

DARES

69 Pair up with a partner and do a "pull-spin." You do a pull-spin by holding hands, facing each other, and spinning around.

70 Crawl on your knees like a horse while another kid rides on your back.

71 Act out your favorite commercial.

 **72** Use the words "balloon," "magnet," and "umbrella" in the same sentence.

 **73** Tell a joke.

74 Stand on one foot with your eyes closed for one full minute.

75 Do ten sit-ups.

 **76** Give someone in the group good advice.

77 Do whatever the youngest person in the group tells you to do.

78 Lie on the floor and sputter and move as if you were a piece of bacon frying in a pan.

DARES

79 Pick someone to be the (pretend) photographer and you pose like a model for a whole roll of pictures. Click! Click! Click!

80 Act like an aerobics instructor and lead the group in five minutes of aerobic exercise.

81 Act out your favorite sport. Let the group guess it. The person who guesses correctly gets to pick the next "It."

82 Pretend someone in the group is your parent and convince him or her to let you sleep over at a friend's house for the weekend.

DARES

83 Act out one of your skills or talents. Let the group guess it. The first person who guesses correctly gets to pick the next "It."

84 Sing your favorite song the way the recording artist does.

DARES

 **85** Recite a line from your favorite movie.

86 Act out your favorite animal.

87 Stand on your head, do a cartwheel, or do the crab walk.

 DARES

88 Act out something you do on your favorite holiday, and have the group guess what it is. The winner gets to pick the next "It."

89 Recite a poem or phrase holding your tongue with your thumb and finger. Example: "My glass is on the table."

DARES

90 Name three of your faults you would like to change.

91 Describe someone you all know, and have the group guess who it is. The first person to guess the right answer gets to pick the next "It."

DARES

92 Make a face that shows an emotion and let the group guess it. The person who guesses correctly gets to pick the next "It."

93 Draw a smiley face on your big toe.

94 Do a cheer like a cheerleader.

DARES